The Nightingale who Lost her Song

By Lizzie Cantopher

ISBN:
978-1-916529-48-9 (Hardback)
978-1-916529-69-4 (Paperback)
978-1-916529-70-0 (E-book)

Written by Lizzie Cantopher
Illustrated by Sofia Sarria
Layout & design by Lynda Mangoro

The Unbound Press
www.theunboundpress.com

Hey unbound one!

Welcome to this magical book brought to you by The Unbound Press.

At The Unbound Press we believe that when women write freely from the fullest expression of who they are, it can't help but activate a feeling of deep connection and transformation in others. When we come together, we become more and we're changing the world, one book at a time!

This book has been carefully crafted by both the author and publisher with the intention of inspiring you to move ever more deeply into who you truly are.

We hope that this book helps you to connect with your Unbound Self and that you feel called to pass it on to others who want to live a more fully expressed life.

With much love,

Nicola Humber

Founder of The Unbound Press

www.theunboundpress.com

Rose Forrest Sue Bentley
Charli Pete
Sofia Sarria
Annie

Jim Clarke-Coley
Charlotte Mia Rose
Deborah Belica
Mike Byrom

Marie Clough

Karin Beale

Rosie Veneta
Cantopher
Sasha Rachel
Christine Gibson

Follow the footsteps of love and compassion to the truth of life.

Once you remember how powerful you are, you will never feel insecure again.

Sue Upton
Chris Jonson
Deb Griffiths
September

Cami Boyett
Pema Chodron
Mark Holmes
Helen Stelitano

Khalil Gibran
Sam Butcher
Arthur Rackham
Martine Batki

Thank you to these amazing souls

Love yourself so deeply

Find the truth of who you really are.

Never give up on yourself

Truth, love, devotion to your own soul.

Susan Clayson

Judith Clayson

Sarah Lloyd
Lynda Mangoro
Nicola Humber
Em Mulholland
Anna Bromley

Allow the wisdom from the universe to stimulate your mind.

Be truthful to your self.

Listen to your heart, then live by your own rhythm.

Dance, sing, laugh out loud.

Be brave, find help.

I would like to dedicate this book to my Great Grandmother, Eliza Pettit,
Who couldn't read or write.

To my children, Charli and Pete,
Who I absolutely adore.
Who overcame their neurodiversities and went to university.

I feel honoured to have watched the change in progress in our family's
educational journey through these beautiful people.

Two creatures were drawn
together one day,

as the wind blew north through the forest clearing.

Minding her own business, and moving at a
glacial pace, walked a large brown bear, as
she shifted from paw to paw, feeling the warm
moss beneath her feet.

She noticed a tiny nightingale sitting
on a low branch, crying.

Normally, the birds flew away and the other
creatures ran for their lives when Bear walked
through the forest; they were so fearful of being
eaten or trampled on by her big paws.

Bear stopped and looked up at Nightingale wiping tears away with her wing.

Very carefully, Bear moved towards the tiny bird sitting on the bough of the big old oak tree.

'Whatever is the matter?' said Bear, in the softest voice she could find.

Nightingale looked around and saw the enormous
creature standing right in front of her.

She stopped and stared down at the bear from her
branch, then continued to cry.

'What has happened to you, my dear?' asked Bear.

Pausing again, with tears falling down her cheeks and
running off her tiny feathers onto the forest floor below,

Nightingale mumbled,
'I have, I have...'

'What have you...? Tell me.'

The tiny bird folded both her wings
over her eyes and cried very softly
which made Bear very sad.

"How can I help you?' said Bear,
And then waited for the little
bird to find her breath.

The bird explained
tearfully,

'I had it. I had it yesterday.
I had it the day before,
but I can't find it today.
Today it's gone.
I can't find it anywhere.
Oh, what am I to do?'

She began to sob.

'What did you lose?' asked Bear, now quite perplexed.

In a small voice, she said, 'I lost my...'

More tears fell down her feathers onto the branch.

She wiped them away, trying her hardest to pull herself together.

The bear, being big and brave stood very still, waiting patiently for
Nightingale to speak.

The tiny bird caught her
breath for a moment
and said with a gush
of tears, 'My song.
My lovely song.

It's gone, disappeared, vanished
without a trace.
I had it yesterday afternoon
just before dusk
before the storm came,
but then it disappeared
and all I'm left with is a bark
and my tiny speaking voice.'

'Show me. Try and sing,' said the kindly bear,
thinking it might help.

And so, Nightingale lifted her head, wiped away her tears, opened her beak, coughed, and tried to sing.

Nothing. Absolutely nothing came out of her beak.

'See what I mean?' she squeaked.

'Yes indeed,' said Bear.
'I do see what you mean.
It has certainly disappeared.
This cannot do, for the forest needs you.
It needs your song.
It needs you to sing each night, especially
now as springtime has just begun.
Would you like me to help you find it?'

'Yes, please.'

Nightingale wiped away her tears as fast as she could to show that she was really quite brave, yet she wasn't at all brave and felt very sad.

Bear continued to ask questions trying to find the facts about the missing songs.

'Did you lose it in the rain last night?'

'I don't think so,' replied Nightingale.

'I started crying when I couldn't find my voice this morning.'

The brown bear decided they should make a plan.

'I think we need to retrace your steps.'

She gently handed the tiniest flower petal she had gathered from the forest floor to Nightingale, so she could wipe away her tears.

Bear said, 'I know what we will do.

We will visit everyone you met yesterday and this morning to see if you may have left your singing voice with them.'

Nightingale smiled at this.

'Who did you see first yesterday?'

'I remember I stood on the branch
of the tree overlooking the small
waterfalls near the river. Just where the
salmon jump high over the stones to
get to the top of the river to lay their
eggs. I was chatting to them.'

'This is good,' said Bear.

'We will walk over there, to the place
where you talked to the salmon.'

As they approached the water, Nightingale suddenly realised that all the salmon she had been watching that morning had long gone upstream and so couldn't help.

'That's a pity,' said Bear.

'Not to worry. Let's move on. Where did you go next, my dear?'

'I went to the cave where all the bats gather and chat before falling asleep amongst the crystals on the cave ceiling.'
So, they decided to visit the bats in the cave.

Nightingale flew beside Bear so they could still see each
other as they followed the moss path to the crystal cave
where the bats slept.

When they arrived at the entrance, Bear softly announced
herself, saying, 'Excuse me,' speaking quietly so as not to
shock or alarm the bats out of their slumber.

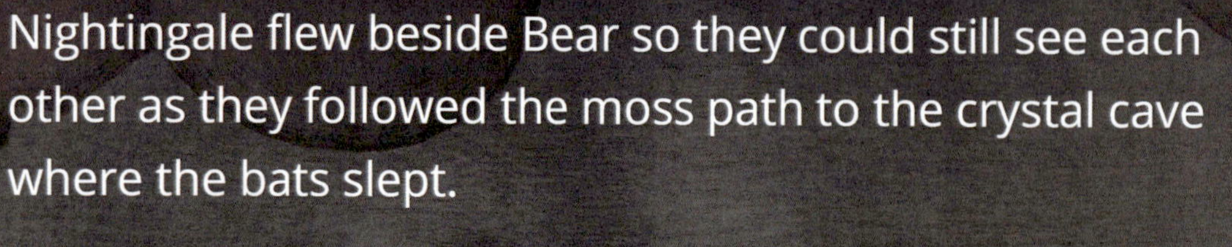

From the darkness of the cave two bright eyes snapped open.

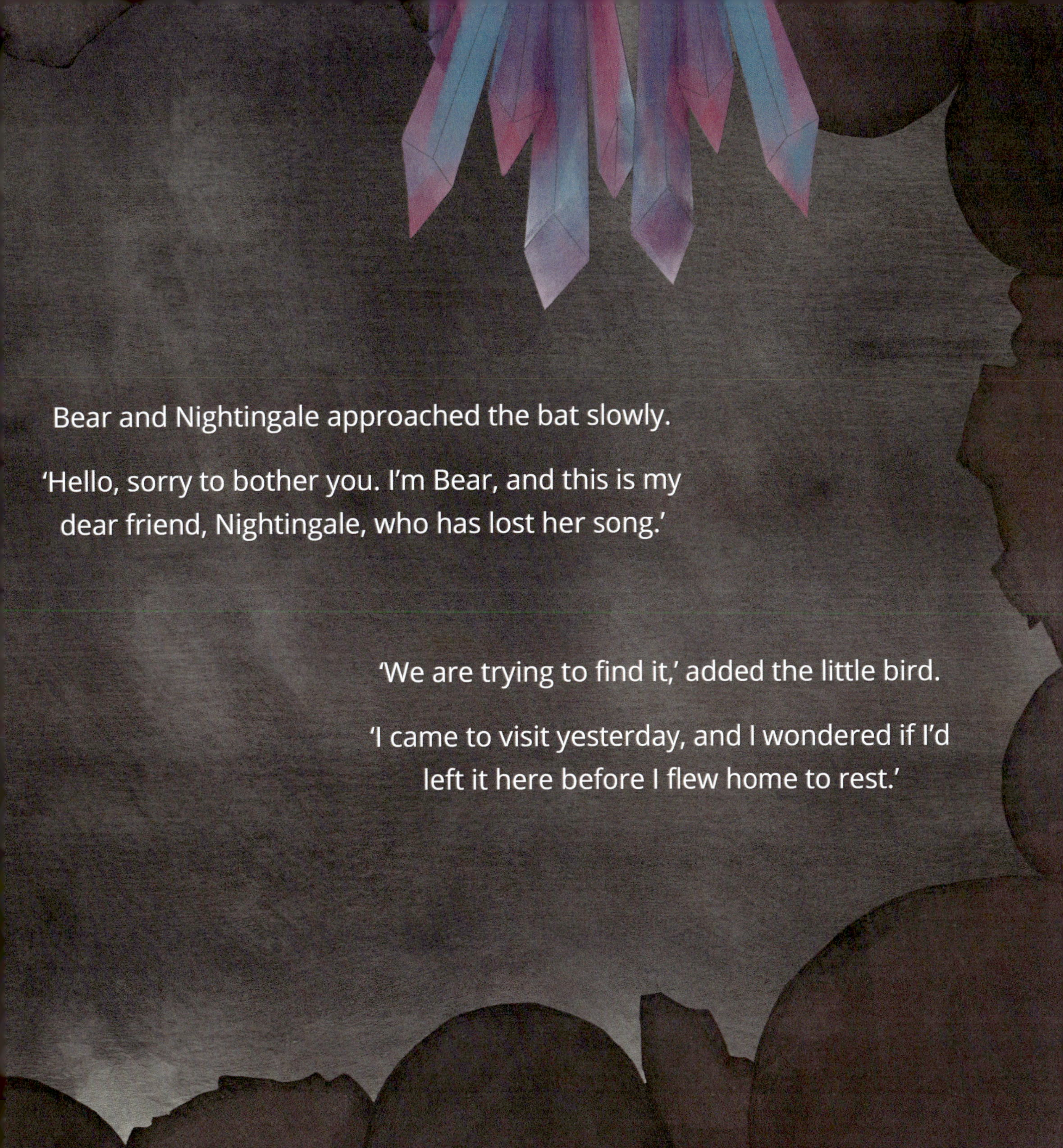

Bear and Nightingale approached the bat slowly.

'Hello, sorry to bother you. I'm Bear, and this is my dear friend, Nightingale, who has lost her song.'

'We are trying to find it,' added the little bird.

'I came to visit yesterday, and I wondered if I'd left it here before I flew home to rest.'

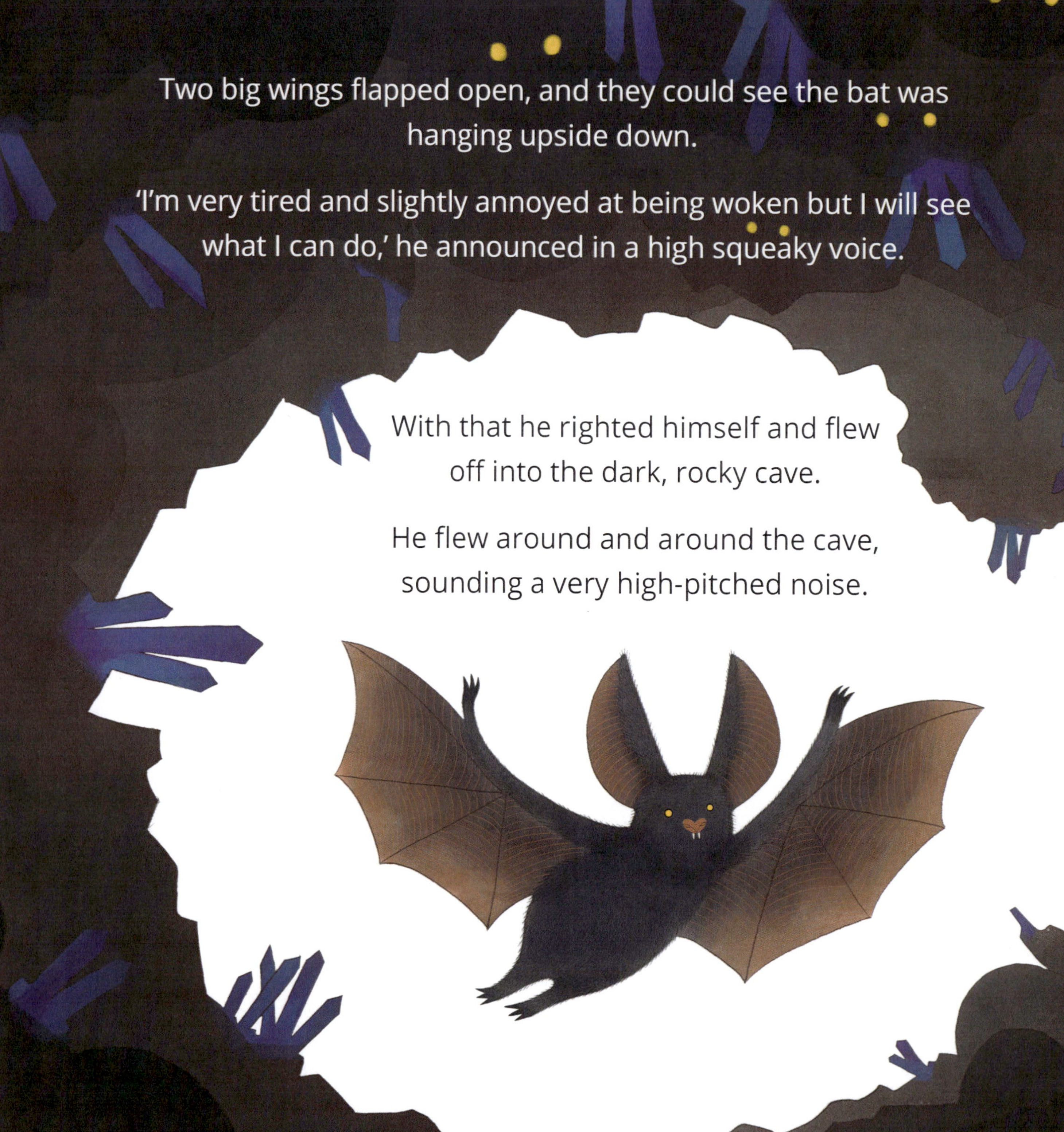

Two big wings flapped open, and they could see the bat was hanging upside down.

'I'm very tired and slightly annoyed at being woken but I will see what I can do,' he announced in a high squeaky voice.

With that he righted himself and flew off into the dark, rocky cave.

He flew around and around the cave, sounding a very high-pitched noise.

Thousands of pairs of eyes simultaneously opened to see Nightingale now standing on top of Bear's head for safety.

The bat called out, 'Ask your question little bird.'

But it was Bear who asked the question.

'My friend, Nightingale seems to have lost her voice, her singing voice. She wondered if she may have left it here? You will recognise it, as it is the most beautiful sound in the forest. Do you know where it is please?'

'Oh yes,' squeaked one of the bats.

'Every night it's exquisite. What a shame you've lost it. I haven't heard it since last night. I love your voice. It sends me to sleep so beautifully.

I heard it last night and that was the last time. I remember falling asleep with a smile on my face, as I felt so happy to be living so close to your beautiful songs. But I don't know where it is now. Has anyone else seen it?'

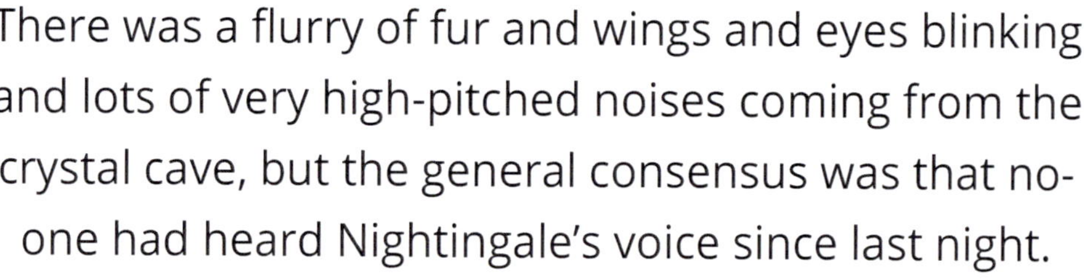

There was a flurry of fur and wings and eyes blinking and lots of very high-pitched noises coming from the crystal cave, but the general consensus was that no-one had heard Nightingale's voice since last night.

The first bat spoke.

'We've not seen or heard your beautiful voice since last night and we're terribly sorry, but we really need to get back to sleep.'

He flew to the ceiling, hooked himself on and hung upside-down.

Thousands of little eyes closed.

Bear and Nightingale stood together for a moment.

Nightingale thought and thought and finally she remembered. She had flown over to see a new gosling on the small pond in the clearing of the forest.

Bear smiled. 'I bet it's there. You jump onto my head, and we will walk through the forest to the clearing.'

So, they set off.

When they got to the small pond, the geese were
all grazing on the grass and popping in and out of
the water to clean their feathers.

Mother Goose was a little surprised to see the huge
brown bear with a small bird on its head.

'Good day to you, Mother Goose,' Bear called out.

'Good day to you too,' called Mother Goose and they both smiled as they knew each other well.

They had a lot of respect for each other too. Bear knew not to wash in the pond while the baby goslings were there, and the goose appreciated this kindness.

'We're on a mission this morning.

We are looking for something that Nightingale has lost,' the bear explained.

'Nightingale!' exclaimed Mother Goose.

'Oh, yes, we love her night-time songs. What did you lose Nightingale?'

The little bird began to say she had lost her singing voice,
but unfortunately, she began to cry again as she was so
tired and deeply sad to have lost her songs.

'Oh, my goodness, dear, don't cry.

I'm sure it's here somewhere.
Let me see if we can find it.

Now, dry those tears and come with us.'

With that, Mother Goose called her young goslings over.

'This is Nightingale, and she has lost her song.

Have any of you seen it or heard it?'

All the goslings thought and thought.

Then one said, 'I remember. I couldn't sleep and you were singing
so sweetly, I felt so relaxed and then I fell fast asleep, thank you.
But, that was the last time I heard your song.'

'We love your songs,' said another gosling.

'But we don't know where your singing voice has gone.
How can we find your song again?'

'Well, maybe we could ask the other creatures who
live near the pond,' replied Bear.

'Maybe they heard it this morning.'

So that is exactly what they did next.

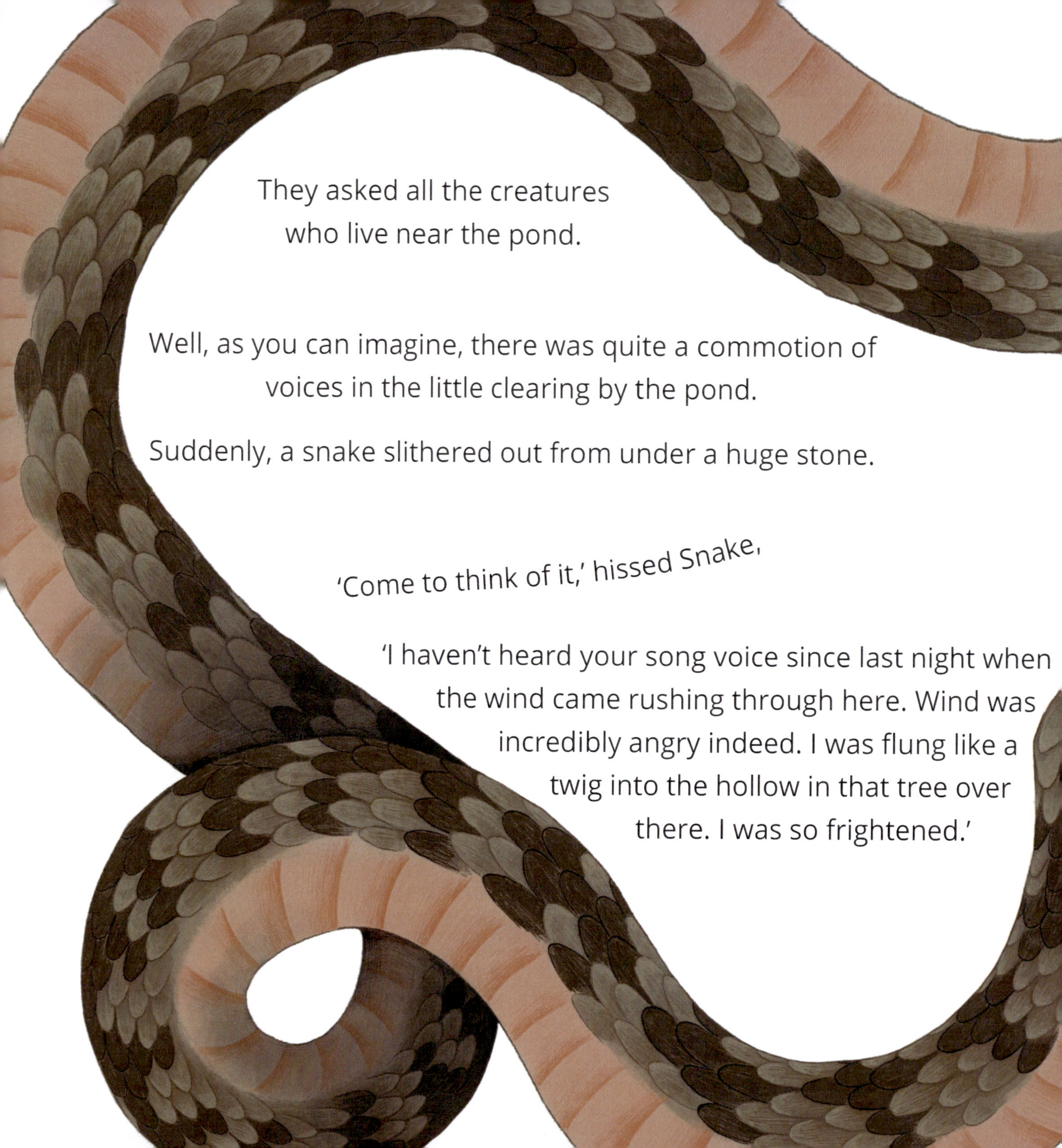

They asked all the creatures
who live near the pond.

Well, as you can imagine, there was quite a commotion of
voices in the little clearing by the pond.

Suddenly, a snake slithered out from under a huge stone.

'Come to think of it,' hissed Snake,

'I haven't heard your song voice since last night when
the wind came rushing through here. Wind was
incredibly angry indeed. I was flung like a
twig into the hollow in that tree over
there. I was so frightened.'

'Yes, that's right,' said Bear.

'Wind was so angry last night; he became an angry storm. He tossed all sorts of things around all over the place.

Then he blew into the tree where Nightingale was singing to close the day ready for night to fall over our forest.'

Nightingale looked at the bear and flew onto a branch.

But, all of a sudden from out of nowhere a large owl flew out of the tree, ruffling up its feathers and squawking loudly.

'What are you all doing near my oak tree?' Owl demanded.

Bear explained what had happened.

The owl said, 'I am shocked by your story, you poor
unfortunate Nightingale.'

'Will you help me find my song?' Nightingale asked.

'Yes of course,' replied the wise old owl.

They all put their heads together for a moment then from out of nowhere a young fawn, with an injured leg came hobbling past the group.

'Excuse me,' she said, politely. 'I overheard you all talking.
If you're looking for the wind, he went south to the river.

He's in a terrible mood. He kicked all sorts of things
up into the air as he pushed past me, and threw a tree
branch at my leg. And it hurts now.'

'What a bully!' called out Snake.

'Let me look at you,' said Mother Goose.

She bent to look at the fawn's leg.

'Oh, my dear, you have a nasty splinter in your leg. Are you brave enough to
let me pull it out with my beak?'

'I'm not very brave, but it does hurt me, so if you wouldn't mind pulling it out,
I would be very grateful. I can't reach it myself,' answered the little deer.

Mother Goose got herself into position then ran towards the faun,
grabbed the exposed splinter of wood hanging from the fawn's
back leg and pulled it clean out.

The little goslings all shouted, 'Hooray!' as their mother spat out
the wood from her beak then went back to inspect.

The fawn gently moved its leg and found the pain had gone.

'Thank you so much.'

'You're very welcome, my dear.

Will you join us to help find
Nightingale's song?'

'Yes of course,' replied the fawn.

Bear asked the fawn, 'What did you see when the wind came through last night?'

The fawn replied gracefully, 'I saw the wind coming, so I knelt on the ground very quickly so it could pass over me.

But it was too quick and before I could get to the floor, he started throwing things around.

I saw Nightingale and heard her singing in the oak tree.
She's usually there at night but she was blown off her perch
into the air for a moment, then landed on her head on the
branch. I saw her beak was wide open with the shock.

I could see the tune falling out of her mouth, as a nearby
crow happened to get blown backwards in the terrible wind.'

'Oh, my goodness!' Nightingale cried.

'I did. I fell over. I hit my head. I can't remember what
happened next. I thought I had fallen asleep.'

'Thank goodness you didn't hurt yourself,' a high voice called out.

It was one of the bats who was now resting upside down in the hollow of the oak tree next to the owl.

Bear said, 'Perhaps the crow swallowed it, by accident.'

'But where is Crow now?' asked Nightingale. The fawn replied, 'I saw him being taken off by the wind.'

'Well, we know who we must find now,' said Snake.

'Who?' asked Owl.

'Who indeed?' said Bear.

'The wind itself,' replied Snake.

'Together we can tackle such a ferocious thing.'

'I will lead,' announced Bear. 'Let's get ready and we will go south, where the river starts.'

And that's exactly what they did.

It took them two whole days to get to the river. They walked and flew in a line, chatting and getting to know each other.

Snake asked nicely at the beginning if she could rest on Bear's back, as it would take her longer to keep up with them all.

The big brown bear was kind enough to accept
Snake, as long as she promised not to sink her
teeth into the bear's fur. Snake promised.

They came to the river, and ahead they saw some old wooden buildings and above was a big angry cloud hovering menacingly.

As the small group approached the edge of the water, the cloud turned and noticed the little animals, then pulled his mouth together and started to blow his cheeks in and out, ready to blow them away.

They all quickly hid in the wooden huts, except Bear, who
was far too fearless for her own good.

Bear roared at Wind and
demanded he explain what
was going on.

Wind was taken aback, and nearly choked on his own puff.

He stormed back, 'How dare you shout at me, Bear?'

The bear replied, 'I dare because you are frightening all the animals.'

Wind blinked a couple of times. And for the first time in his life, he was so shocked he could hardly speak; just a few tiny puffs of cloud fell from his mouth.

But this wasn't acceptable to Bear.

She shouted again at Wind.

The snake, still clinging to the bear's brown fur, fell to the ground in fear of its life and curled up under a stone.

Bear realising Snake was frightened, and without taking her eyes off the storm, said gently,

'Oh, I am sorry, Snake. I'm not shouting at you. There's no need to be scared but definitely stay under that stone.'

Then Wind blew out the words, 'Well Bear, you have my full attention. What do you want?'

Bear gathered the right words to say in her mind and now she only had a few seconds to say them before the wind changed its mind.

With her most commanding deep and controlled voice she called out,

'My dear friend, Nightingale had the most beautiful voice until a few nights ago. She was knocked off her perch and hit her head on an old branch from the oak tree in the forest, after you had rushed past with your terrible temper. We have been looking everywhere for her singing voice, trying to retrace her steps. Quite frankly, she is very sad. No creature should have to go through this because of someone else rushing past in a stormy temper and taking something that doesn't belong to them.'

At this, Wind looked menacingly at Bear, but she continued, 'I'd like to know if you are hiding Nightingale's singing voice in your Wind formation as we can't find it anywhere.

Can you shed some light on this?

What are you going to do?'

There was a pause. The whole of the forest was holding its breath.

Wind blinked a couple of times, looking down at the bear and then shook his head from side to side.

Wind couldn't believe that anything would talk to him in this way, everybody had always been so frightened of him.

Once again Wind blinked a couple of times, looked directly at the bear, and said, with a trembling bottom lip, 'I'm...'

And then Wind rushed from side to side, puffing himself up.

Bear shouted at the stormy cloud.

'Don't you dare be so puffed up!
Don't you dare rush away!'

'I'm trying to find it!

I'm trying, I'm trying to find it,'
Wind called.

'Please try and be patient.'

Leaves and pebbles and
stones tumbled out of the
clouds as he searched
for the nightingale's
sweet song.

Then butterflies and nests and broken branches spilled out.

Flashes of lightning and drops of rain flew out. And then all of a sudden, with a loud squawk, a large black crow rolled out of the clouds and landed on the back of the brown bear.

'Don't be alarmed,' called Bear.

'I won't hurt you.'

'Oh, thank goodness!' exclaimed the crow.

'It's been terrible. I've been up all night.

I'm exhausted.

Wind rolled me up inside his stormy clouds. He stole me and kept me prisoner.'

The little nightingale flew to Crow.

'You poor thing. You
must have been
terrified.

'I'm Nightingale. I lost my voice when Wind was storming through the forest last night. Have you got my singing voice?'

The crow shook his feathers and pulled himself together and called out.

'I did have your voice, but he stole it from me. He has your voice. Wind has Nightingale's voice. I heard it. I heard it in the middle of the storm.'

Everyone knows that crows cannot
lie, and Bear and Nightingale now
stared up at Wind.

At that moment, Wind shouted down,

'I feel lonely up here on my own without a friend.
I collect things: objects, creatures, flowers, and I
keep them, so I don't feel alone anymore.'

'Show me!' Bear ordered.

'Send everything out so I can see all you have collected.'

Wind blinked again with his big black eyes.

He said, sadly, 'I didn't mean it. I couldn't help it. I was angry.
I don't know why I've been so angry.'

Rain started to pour from the clouds and lightning flashed
from each of his eyes.

Bear called out, waving her huge paws at Wind, 'Stop that. Calm down. You're not in trouble.

We just need to find the things and get them back to where they belong.'

Crow then told everyone how Wind had taken away all sorts of things from the surrounding area without a care in the world, and how he just pulled them up into the clouds himself and threw them out at any time he liked.

While caught in the middle of the stormy wind, trying desperately to get away without any success, Crow had held onto the song.

But all the tumbling around inside the storm forced Nightingale's song to fly from his beak and into a hollow log.

'It may still be trapped inside that log,' cried Crow.

Bear thanked Crow for being so brave. 'Sometimes we have to do what is right and stop what is going wrong.'

She turned to Wind. 'Hand over the log, please. The log with Nightingale's voice inside it.'

'No!' cried Wind. 'I want it. It gives me comfort.'

'You cannot have what is not yours. Hand it over, please.'

Wind said, miserably, 'I can't hear the song anymore. It was so beautiful.'

Nightingale then
had an idea and
whispered into
Bear's ear.

Bear nodded and smiled.

Bear addressed Wind.

'Nightingale's singing voice you trapped inside a hollow log has stopped.

We think the reason you can't hear it any longer is because it's not in the right place.

Throw the log out to us, and Nightingale will look to see if she can find the voice inside the log.'

Nightingale added, 'If you release my singing voice, I will sing to you every day and every night for as long as I live.'

Wind blinked away his tears.

'I love hearing the voice and I really do miss it. I would love nothing more than to return to being an ordinary big white puffy cloud that only rains on the land when it needs it.

I don't really want to be angry anymore, so I'll go and have a look.'

Wind started to move and roll and pushed himself inside out.

Pieces of wood, huge plants, feathers and mushrooms flew out. Even a tiny green frog jumped out of the clouds and hopped onto a lily pad.

Wind started to cry which meant more rain.

For good manners, Wind moved over the top of the lake so it wouldn't soak everyone.

'I will count to three', said Bear patiently.

'And on the count of three, you will send the log with the voice in it down to the land.'

Calmly Bear added, 'Send it carefully so we can see if Nightingale's voice is in there. Are you ready?'

Wind, still crying a little, nodded and moved over towards them again.

The ground of the forest was happy to have extra water to feed the plants.

'ONE...TWO...THREE!

And
on three, the
small, very wet log shot

out of Wind's mouth and landed square
on the floor with a thud right
next to Bear.

Bear said, 'Everyone, come and
gather around so the sound does
not escape into thin air.'

All of the creatures did so, and Nightingale jumped onto the log.

Snake slithered onto the small log and found her way into a tiny hole, using her forked tongue to smell the delicious taste of sweet melodies within the log.

Snake opened her mouth, wide, and silently consumed the sound. She slid out of another split in the wood and found her way back to Bear.

Nightingale stood waiting on the log.

'Nightingale,' said Snake.

'Don't be frightened. I will not eat you. Open your mouth I will return your song to you.'

The tiny bird opened her beak and Snake,

in one movement, dislodged her jaw and regurgitated the voice in one whole block of sound into Nightingale.

Everyone was silent as Nightingale swallowed the sound down.

The creatures waited to see what would happen as the little bird ruffled her feathers, flapped her wings, and puffed a small, amount of wind from her lungs.

She tapped her chest with her wings and apologised with a smile. Then she flew up into the oak tree, assumed her normal position, and opened her beak to sing.

She tried again, but to her dismay no song came out.

Then she thought of something, and announced, 'I'd like to dedicate this next song, to Wind, who we all know has a stormy temper but doesn't really mean any harm.'

She looked down at all the creatures, including the goslings who had been so well-behaved on this field trip. They all waited for the little bird to open her beak and sing once again.

With a little cough and jiggle of her feathers, Nightingale started to sing.

Her song was so pure, all the creatures were in tears.

Wind once again moved over the lake so he could cry happy tears without anyone getting too wet.

With tears in her eyes, tears of love, and with love in her heart, the more she sang the sweeter her voice became.

All looked, and even the flowers turned their heads up towards the branch where Nightingale stood.

Bear felt so proud of her little brave friend.

Nightingale thanked all who had been part of her journey to find her singing voice.

She told them they had been so special to her they would be forever in her heart, and she would now be singing every single day and night for the rest of her life in the beautiful forest.

And with that, she burst once more into song.

Wind, now losing his dark shadowy sides, began to smile as the sun burst through him.

And the day became full and
rich with love and friendship
happiness, and the sound o
joy everywhere.

About the Author

This is Lizzie Cantopher's first book. Before 2024, Lizzie didn't tell many people she had dyslexia. She went to an ordinary school, and she was told from a very young age that she was a bit stupid because she didn't read and write the same as everyone else.

At age 67, she decided it was time to stand in her own truth. In a local bookshop she found a shelf of books that she could finally read. It was the bookshop owner, who suggested to Lizzie that she should write her story, and the very next day the story of the Nightingale began to flood onto the page.

For years, Lizzie managed to hide her superpower, through asking for help and sheer tenacity – navigating a successful nursing career, motherhood, becoming a property investor and eventually finding love with her partner Annie.

But now the secret is out. Lizzie hopes to inspire others who process and learn differently. That they are not alone and that they can turn the impossible into possible.

You can find more about Lizzie on www.lizziecantopher.com

www.ingramcontent.com/pod-product-compliance
Lightning Source LLC
Chambersburg PA
CBRC092147180726
48295CB00009B/135